Auntie Loves You!

For Sarah Rockett, super editor and aunt, and for Bob.
—Helen Foster James

In memory of Jan
—Petra Brown

Sleeping Bear Press™

2395 South Huron Parkway, Suite 200
Ann Arbor, MI 48104
www.sleepingbearpress.com

Printed and bound in the United States.

10 9 8

Library of Congress Cataloging-in-Publication Data

Names: James, Helen Foster, 1951- author. | Brown, Petra, illustrator.
Title: Auntie loves you! / written by Helen Foster James;
illustrated by Petra Brown.
Description: Ann Arbor, MI : Sleeping Bear Press, [2018] | Summary:
Illustrations and simple, rhyming text celebrate the special relationship
between a rabbit and the baby who made her an aunt.
Identifiers: LCCN 2018014173 | ISBN 9781534110113
Subjects: | CYAC: Stories in rhyme. | Aunts–Fiction.
| Babies–Fiction. | Rabbits–Fiction.
Classification: LCC PZ8.3.J1477 Aun 2018 | DDC [E]–dc23
LC record available at https://lccn.loc.gov/2018014173

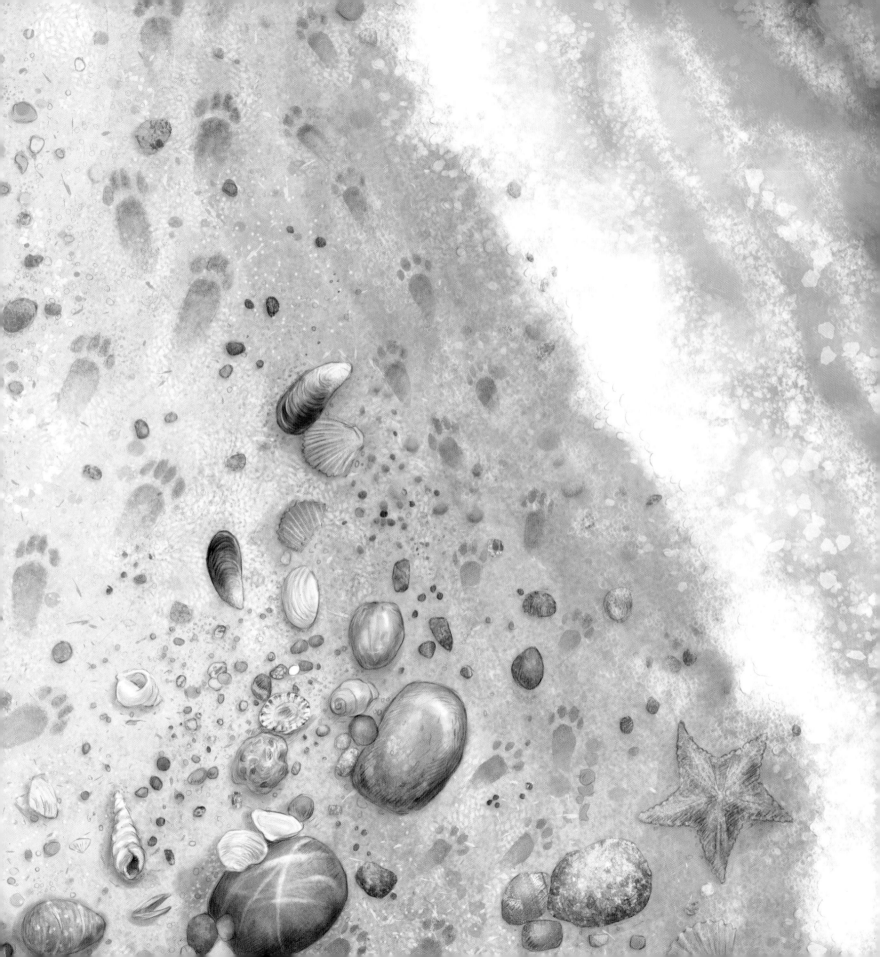

This book is presented to:

Charlie Connell + Baby C

On this day:

February 6, 2021

Auntie

Written by Helen Foster James

Loves You!

Illustrated by Petra Brown

The moment we met
I knew you would be,

bunny-kins bunny,
a treasure to me.

We'll be best buddies
like carrots and peas,

like beaches and sand,
or seashells and seas.

My funny bunny,
we'll dance and we'll sing.

We'll make up new games.
We'll slide and we'll swing.

Sugar-pie sweetie,
we'll hippity-hop.

We'll binky with joy,
and flippity-flop.

We go together
like sprinkles on cake,

like kisses and hugs,
or ducks on a lake.

We'll make yummy treats,
and have lots of fun,

laughing and playing
until our day's done.

My heart's full of love
and I hope you know,

my love goes with you
wherever you go.

Your auntie loves you!
Now, nighty-night-night.

Snuggle down, bunny.
Sleep tight, love, sleep tight.

A Special Letter
to My Favorite Bunny

Somewhere 6,791 kilometers away
your Aunty Christie is sitting and
missing you. Please always
remember how much you are
each loved. You bring so much
joy to your Aunty's life. Sometime
soon we will all be together again.
For now, be good for your mom + dad.
With Love, Aunty Christie

Paste a picture of auntie

and child here.

This will remain blank until
our newest love bug is
with us. ♡